D1827019

Benjamin Britten

SENTIMENTAL SARABAND
from 'Simple Symphony'

arranged for piano duet by
Howard Ferguson

Oxford University Press
Music Department · 44 Conduit Street · London WıR ODE

1. 40

SENTIMENTAL SARABAND

BENJAMIN BRITTEN
arranged by Howard Ferguson

† From Suite No. 3 (for piano), 1925.

© Oxford University Press 1972

Printed in Great Britain

OXFORD UNIVERSITY PRESS, MUSIC DEPARTMENT, 44 CONDUIT STREET, LONDON, W1R 0DE

Sentimental Saraband

Poco più tranquillo

Sentimental Saraband

8

Più agitato

★ The r.h. chord in each part should coincide with the top note of the l.h. arpeggio.

Sentimental Saraband

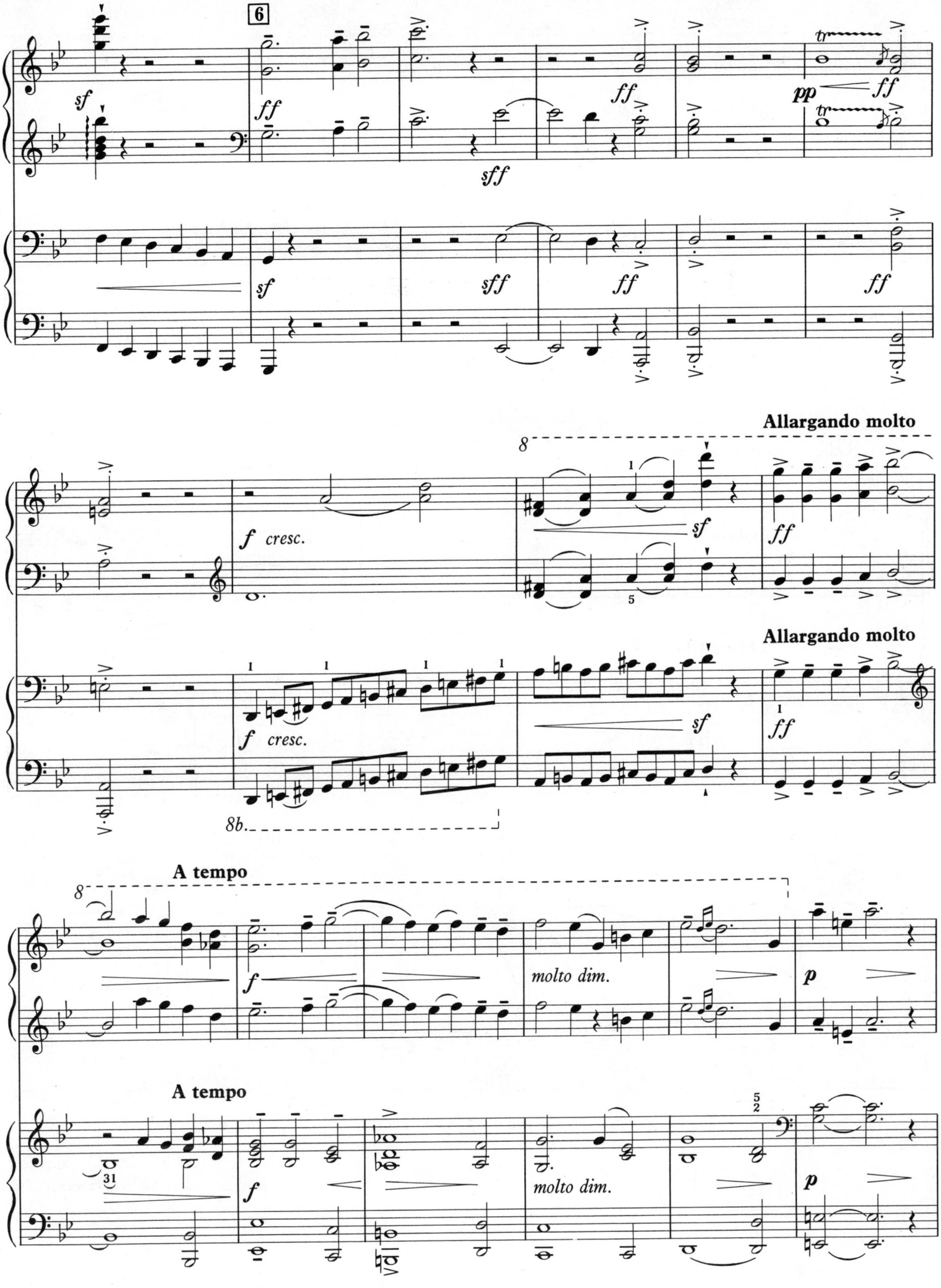
6
sf
ff
sff
tr
pp
Allargando molto
f cresc.
8b.
A tempo
molto dim.
p

Sentimental Saraband

Processed and printed by
Halstan & Co. Ltd., Amersham, Bucks., England